Saint George and the Dragon

Saint George and the Dragon

A Golden Legend Adapted by
Margaret Hodges
from Edmund Spenser's *Faerie Queene*

Illustrated by
Trina Schart Hyman

LITTLE, BROWN *and* COMPANY

BOSTON

TORONTO

Library of Congress Cataloging in Publication Data

Hodges, Margaret.
    Saint George and the dragon.

    Summary: Retells the segment from Spenser's The
Faerie Queene, in which George, the Red Cross Knight,
slays the dreadful dragon that has been terrorizing the
countryside for years and brings peace and joy to the
land.
    1. George, Saint, d. 303—Legends. [1. George,
Saint, d. 303. 2. Folklore—England. 3. Knights and
knighthood—Fiction. 4. Dragons—Fiction] I. Hyman,
Trina Schart, ill. II. Spenser, Edmund, 1552?–1599.
Faerie queene. III. Title.
PZ8.1.H69Sai 1984   [398.2]   83–19980
ISBN 0–316–36789–3

Second Printing

AHS

*Published simultaneously in Canada
by Little, Brown & Company (Canada) Limited*

PRINTED IN THE UNITED STATES OF AMERICA

To Bob and Jan Hinman
in memory of a feast of feasts
the night of the reading
and of the George and Dragon puppets

M.H.

To Hilary Knight, with love

T.S.H.

IN THE DAYS when monsters and giants and fairy folk lived in England, a noble knight was riding across a plain. He wore heavy armor and carried an ancient silver shield marked with a red cross. It was dented with the blows of many battles fought long ago by other brave knights.

The Red Cross Knight had never yet faced a foe, and did not even know his name or where he had been born. But now he was bound on a great adventure, sent by the Queen of the Fairies to try his young strength against a deadly enemy, a dragon grim and horrible.

Beside him, on a little white donkey, rode a princess leading a white lamb, and behind her came a dwarf carrying a small bundle of food. The lady's lovely face was veiled and her shoulders were covered with a black cloak, as if she had a hidden sorrow in her heart. Her name was Una.

The dreadful dragon was the cause of her sorrow. He was laying waste to her land so that many frightened people had left their homes and run away. Others had shut themselves inside the walls of a castle with Una's father and mother, the king and queen of the country. But Una had set out alone from the safety of the castle walls to look for a champion who would face the terrible dragon. She had traveled a long, long way before she found the Red Cross Knight.

Like a sailor long at sea, under stormy winds and fierce sun, who begins to whistle merrily when he sees land, so Una was thankful.

Now the travelers rode together, through wild woods and wilderness, perils and dangers, toward Una's kingdom. The path they had to follow was straight and narrow, but not easy to see. Sometimes the Red Cross Knight rode too far ahead of Una and lost his way. Then she had to find him and guide him back to the path. So they journeyed on. With Una by his side, fair and faithful, no monster or giant could stand before the knight's bright sword.

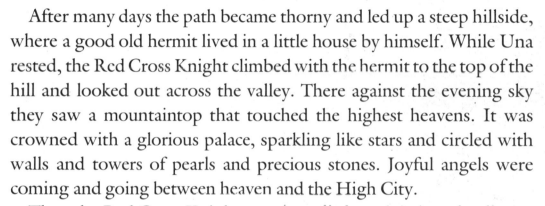

After many days the path became thorny and led up a steep hillside, where a good old hermit lived in a little house by himself. While Una rested, the Red Cross Knight climbed with the hermit to the top of the hill and looked out across the valley. There against the evening sky they saw a mountaintop that touched the highest heavens. It was crowned with a glorious palace, sparkling like stars and circled with walls and towers of pearls and precious stones. Joyful angels were coming and going between heaven and the High City.

Then the Red Cross Knight saw that a little path led up the distant mountain to that city, and he said, "I thought that the fairest palace in the world was the crystal tower in the city of the Fairy Queen. Now I see a palace far more lovely. Una and I should go there at once."

But the old hermit said, "The Fairy Queen has sent you to do brave deeds in this world. That High City that you see is in another world. Before you climb the path to it and hang your shield on its wall, go down into the valley and fight the dragon that you were sent to fight.

11

"It is time for me to tell you that you were not born of fairy folk, but of English earth. The fairies stole you away as a baby while you slept in your cradle. They hid you in a farmer's field, where a plowman found you. He called you George, which means 'Plow the Earth' and 'Fight the Good Fight.' For you were born to be England's friend and patron saint, Saint George of Merry England."

Then George, the Red Cross Knight, returned to Una, and when morning came, they went together down into the valley. They rode through farmlands, where men and women working in their fields looked up and cheered because a champion had come to fight the dragon, and children clapped their hands to see the brave knight and the lovely lady ride by.

"Now we have come to my own country," said Una. "Be on your guard. See, there is the city and the great brass tower that my parents built strong enough to stand against the brassy-scaled dragon. There are my father and mother looking out from the walls, and the watch-man stands at the top, waiting to call out the good news if help is coming."

Then they heard a hideous roaring that filled the air with terror and seemed to shake the ground. The dreadful dragon lay stretched on the sunny side of a great hill, like a great hill himself, and when he saw the knight's armor glistening in the sunlight, he came eagerly to do battle. The knight bade his lady stand apart, out of danger, to watch the fight, while the beast drew near, half flying, half running. His great size made a wide shadow under his huge body as a mountain casts a shadow on a valley. He reared high, monstrous, horrible, and vast, armed all over with scales of brass fitted so closely that no sword or spear could pierce them. They clashed with every movement. The dragon's wings stretched out like two sails when the wind fills them. The clouds fled before him. His huge, long tail, speckled red and black, wound in a hundred folds over his scaly back and swept the land behind him for almost half a mile. In his tail's end, two sharp stings were fixed. But sharper still were <u>his</u> cruel claws. Whatever he touched or drew within those claws was in deadly danger. His head was more hideous than tongue can tell, for his deep jaws gaped wide, showing three rows of iron teeth ready to devour his prey. A cloud of smothering smoke and burning sulfur poured from his throat, filling the air with its stench. His blazing eyes, flaming with rage, glared out from deep in his head. So he came toward the knight, raising his speckled breast, clashing his scales, as he leaped to greet his newest victim.

The knight on horseback fiercely rode at the dragon with all his might and couched his spear, but as they passed, the pointed steel glanced off the dragon's hard hide. The wrathful beast, surprised at the strength of the blow, turned quickly, and, passing the knight again, brushed him with his long tail so that horse and man fell to the ground.

Once more the Red Cross Knight mounted and attacked the dragon. Once more in vain. Yet the beast had never before felt such a mighty stroke from the hand of any man, and he was furious for revenge. With his waving wings spread wide, he lifted himself high from the ground, then, stooping low, snatched up both horse and man to carry them away. High above the plain he bore them as far as a bow can shoot an arrow, but even then the knight still struggled until the monster was forced to lower his paws so that both horse and rider fought free. With the strength of three men, again the knight struck. The spear glanced off the scaly neck, but it pierced the dragon's left wing, spread broad above him, and the beast roared like a raging sea in a winter storm. Furious, he snatched the spear in his claws and broke it off, throwing forth flames of fire from his nostrils. Then he hurled his hideous tail about and wrapped it around the legs of the horse, until, striving to loose the knot, the horse threw its rider to the ground.

Quickly the knight rose. He drew his sharp sword and struck the dragon's head so fiercely that it seemed nothing could withstand the blow. The dragon's crest was too hard to take a cut, but he wanted no more such blows. He tried to fly away and could not because of his wounded wing.

Loudly he bellowed—the like was never heard before—and from his body, like a wide devouring oven, sent a flame of fire that scorched the knight's face and heated his armor red-hot. Faint, weary, sore, burning with heat and wounds, the knight fell to the ground, ready to die, and the dragon clapped his iron wings in victory, while the lady, watching from afar, fell to her knees. She thought that her champion had lost the battle.

But it happened that where the knight fell, an ancient spring of silvery water bubbled from the ground. In that cool water the knight lay resting until the sun rose. Then he, too, rose to do battle again. And when the dragon saw him, he could hardly believe his eyes. Could this be the same knight, he wondered, or another who had come to take his place?

The knight brandished his bright blade, and it seemed sharper than ever, his hands even stronger. He smote the crested head with a blow so mighty that the dragon reared up like a hundred raging lions. His long, stinging tail threw down high trees and tore rocks to pieces. Lashing forward, it pierced the knight's shield and its point stuck fast in his shoulder. He tried to free himself from that barbed sting, but when he saw that his struggles were in vain, he raised his fighting sword and struck a blow that cut off the end of the dragon's tail.

Heart cannot think what outrage and what cries, with black smoke and flashing fire, the beast threw forth, turning the whole world to darkness. Gathering himself up, wild for revenge, he fiercely fell upon the sunbright shield and gripped it fast with his paws. Three times the knight tried and failed to pull the shield free. Then, laying about him with his trusty sword, he struck so many blows that fire flew from the dragon's coat like sparks from an anvil, and the beast raised one paw to defend himself. Striking with might and main, the knight severed the other paw, which still clung to the shield.

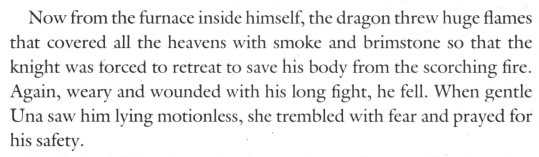

Now from the furnace inside himself, the dragon threw huge flames that covered all the heavens with smoke and brimstone so that the knight was forced to retreat to save his body from the scorching fire. Again, weary and wounded with his long fight, he fell. When gentle Una saw him lying motionless, she trembled with fear and prayed for his safety.

But he had fallen beneath a fair apple tree, its spreading branches covered with red fruit, and from that tree dropped a healing dew that the deadly dragon did not dare to come near. Once more the daylight faded and night spread over the earth. Under the apple tree the knight slept.

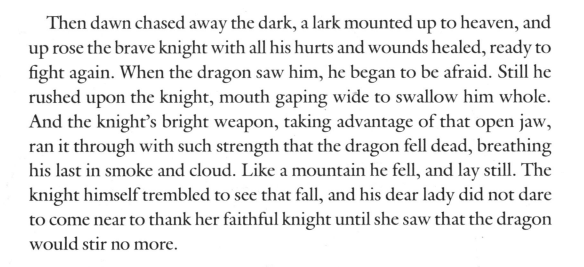

Then dawn chased away the dark, a lark mounted up to heaven, and up rose the brave knight with all his hurts and wounds healed, ready to fight again. When the dragon saw him, he began to be afraid. Still he rushed upon the knight, mouth gaping wide to swallow him whole. And the knight's bright weapon, taking advantage of that open jaw, ran it through with such strength that the dragon fell dead, breathing his last in smoke and cloud. Like a mountain he fell, and lay still. The knight himself trembled to see that fall, and his dear lady did not dare to come near to thank her faithful knight until she saw that the dragon would stir no more.

Now our ship comes into port. Furl the sails and drop anchor.
Safe from storm, Una is at her journey's end.

The watchman on the castle wall called out to the king and queen that the dragon was dead, and when the old king saw that it was true, he ordered the castle's great brass gates to be opened so that the tidings of peace and joy might spread through all the land. Trumpets sounded the news that the great beast had fallen. Then the king and queen came out of the city with all their nobles to meet the Red Cross Knight. Tall young men led the way, carrying laurel branches to lay at the hero's feet. Pretty girls wore wreaths of flowers and made music on tambourines. The children came dancing, laughing and singing, with a crown of flowers for Una. They gazed in wonder at the victorious knight.

But when the people saw where the dead dragon lay, they dared not come near to touch him. Some ran away, some pretended not to be afraid. One said the dragon might still be alive; one said he saw fire in the eyes. Another said the eyes were moving. When a foolish child ran forward to touch the dragon's claws, his mother scolded him. "How can I tell?" she said. "Those claws might scratch my son, or tear his tender hand." At last some of the bolder men began to measure the dragon to prove how many acres his body covered.

The old king embraced and kissed his daughter. He gave gifts of gold and ivory and a thousand thanks to the dragonslayer. But the knight told the king never to forget the poor people, and gave the rich gifts to them. Then back to the palace all the people went, still singing, to feast and to hear the story of the knight's adventures with Una.

When the tale ended the king said, "Never did living man sail through such a sea of deadly dangers. Since you are now safely come to shore, stay here and live happily ever after. You have earned your rest."

But the brave knight answered, "No, my lord, I have sworn to give knight's service to the Fairy Queen for six years. Until then, I cannot rest."

The king said, "I have promised that the dragonslayer should have Una for his wife, and be king after me. If you love each other, my daughter is yours now. My kingdom shall be yours when you have done your service for the Fairy Queen and returned to us."

Then he called Una, who came no longer wearing her black cloak and her veil, but dressed in a lily-white gown that shimmered like silver. Never had the knight seen her so beautiful. Whenever he looked at the brightness of her sunshiny face, his heart melted with pleasure.

So Una and the Red Cross Knight were married and lived together joyfully. But the knight did not forget his promise to serve the Fairy Queen, and when she called him into service, off he rode on brave adventures, until at last he earned his name, Saint George of Merry England.

That is how it is when jolly sailors come into a quiet harbor. They unload their cargo, mend ship, and take on fresh supplies. Then away they sail on another long voyage, while we are left on shore, waving good-bye and wishing them Godspeed.